Percy's Chocolate Crunch
and other Thomas the Tank Engine Stories

Random House 🏠 **New York**
A Random House PICTUREBACK® Book
Photographs by David Mitton, Terry Palone, and Terry Permane for
Britt Allcroft's production of *Thomas the Tank Engine and Friends*.

Thomas the Tank Engine & Friends A BRITT ALLCROFT COMPANY PRODUCTION Based on The Railway Series by The Rev W Awdry
Copyright © 2003 Gullane (Thomas) LLC.   Photographs © 2003 Gullane (Thomas) Limited.
All rights reserved under International and Pan-American Copyright Conventions. Published in the United States by Random House Children's Books,
a division of Random House, Inc., New York, and simultaneously in Canada by Random House of Canada Limited, Toronto.
www.randomhouse.com/kids   www.thomasthetankengine.com
Library of Congress Cataloging-in-Publication Data
Percy's chocolate crunch: and other Thomas the tank engine stories/ photographs by David Mitton, Terry Palone, and Terry Permane for Britt Allcroft's production of
Thomas the tank engine and friends.   p.   cm.   "Based on The railway series by The Rev. W. Awdry."
CONTENTS: A collection of stories about Percy, Harold the Helicopter, and other friends of Thomas the tank engine.
ISBN 0-375-81392-6   [1. Railroads—Trains—Fiction. 2. Helicopters—Fiction.]
I. Title: Percy's chocolate crunch, and other Thomas the tank engine stories. II. Mitton, David, ill. III. Palone, Terry, ill. IV. Permane, Terry, ill. V. Awdry, W. Railway series. VI.
Thomas the tank engine and friends. PZ7 .P42475 2003 [E]—dc21 2002151585
Printed in the United States of America 20 19 18 17 16 15 14 13
PICTUREBACK, RANDOM HOUSE and colophon, and PLEASE READ TO ME and colophon are registered trademarks of Random House, Inc.

PERCY'S CHOCOLATE CRUNCH

Sir Topham Hatt's engines love being shiny and clean. It makes them feel cheerful as they puff across the Island of Sodor.

Percy often has the dirtiest work to do. But he likes to be clean as well as any other engine. Washdowns are important to Percy.

But Sir Topham Hatt had bad news. "Due to a water shortage," he said, "no engine shall have more than one washdown a day."

"Usefulness before cleanliness," he added. And left.

Percy was upset. "I get dirty," he complained. "I need washdowns. Gordon only does it to feel important."

"I *am* important," Gordon sniffed. "I'm an express engine."

"You're a pouty puffer, Percy," teased James.

"No, I'm not," wheeshed Percy. And he chuffed away.

Percy was loading freight cars at the docks. He was trying extra hard to stay clean. But the Troublesome Trucks were being naughty.

As Percy pushed them under the coal chute, they sang out. "On! On! On!" they cried. Percy found himself under the chute. And coal dust flew everywhere!

"Oh, no!" coughed Percy. "I'm filthy!" Percy felt awful but he knew he had to carry on.

On the way to Callan Station, the Troublesome Trucks teased
Percy even more.

  "Clickety clack.
  Don't look back.
  Dirty Percy's on our track!"
"Be quiet!" Percy snapped.

When Percy arrived at Callan Station, he was very upset. "From now on, I am only doing work where I won't get dirty."

Harold the Helicopter was at Callan Station picking up medical supplies. "Hullo, Percy," he called. And he took off, blowing cinders and ashes everywhere.

"Not again!" cried Percy. "I want a washdown!"

"Usefulness before cleanliness," reminded his driver.

"I want to be useful where I can't get dirty!" Percy huffed.

"There's a load of sugar going to the chocolate factory,"
his driver said. "We could take the sugar cars."
"Sugar," said Percy. "*That's* nice and clean."
Percy was pleased.

Percy didn't know that earlier a leaky freight car had spilled oil on the track. When he approached the chocolate factory, his driver applied the brakes. But Percy's wheels just skidded on the oily rails.

"Oh, no!" hooted Percy. "Yuck!" he groaned. "I've never been *this* dirty!"

He was covered from funnel to firebox in sticky, gooey chocolate.

Back at the sheds, everyone thought it was very funny.

"You look good enough to eat!" Thomas hooted.

"Bonbon Percy," teased James.

"Choc Ice on wheels!" chipped in Henry.

"Disgraceful," said Gordon pompously.

"Ahem!" said a stern-sounding voice. It was Sir Topham Hatt. "You have had a trying day, Percy!" he said.

"Yes, sir," replied Percy from beneath the chocolate.

"But you've showed us all that usefulness does come before cleanliness. So," he added, "you shall have your washdown—"

"Oh, sir!"

"And a new coat of paint!"

Percy just *beamed*!

SALTY'S SECRET

All the engines on the Island of Sodor love their work. But sometimes there is too much work. That's when Sir Topham Hatt brings new engines to the island.

Salty the Dockyard Diesel is one of these engines. He loves to tell tales of the sea.

"... We heaved until the old freighter finally caught the tide. Arrgh, it's good to be useful!"

Salty is excited about coming to the Island of Sodor. Islands are surrounded by the sea. Salty loves the sea.

Soon Salty arrived at his new job. "Ahoy, mateys! Salty, pride of the seven seas. I'm a new diesel, and I'm here to give you some help."

Bill and Ben didn't think they needed any help. Especially from a diesel.

"Welcome to Center Island Quarry," Mavis said proudly.

Salty looked all around. Everywhere he looked he saw
nothing but rocks. "A *quarry*?" he cried. "There must be
some mistake. I'm a dockyard diesel."

"You're a quarry diesel now," Mavis said. And she
explained that they had to complete an important job for
Sir Topham Hatt.

Salty was sad that he wouldn't be working by the sea. But he knew what it meant to be a Really Useful Engine. And he set to work at once.

"Ah, well," Salty said. "At least there be trucks."

"You'd better mind them," Mavis said. "They can be a bother."

"He won't last five minutes," said Bill.

"Those trucks will trip him up soon enough," said Ben.

But to Bill and Ben's surprise, the trucks seemed to give Salty no trouble at all.

> *Yo ho ho and a bucket of prawns. The tiller spins and the captain yawns.*
>
> *Yo ho ho and a bucket of prawns. The tiller spins—"* sang Salty.

"—And the captain yawns," sang the trucks.

Thanks to Salty, Sir Topham Hatt's important job was almost done. Bill and Ben were surprised . . . and a little jealous.

"Here comes Mister Show-off," groused Ben.

"You have to admit he's got a knack with those trucks," said Mavis.

"Driver says he'll bore the bolts off us with his stories," huffed Bill.

But Salty didn't say a word. He didn't come near the shed.

Mavis was worried. She rolled alongside and asked him what he was doing on his own.

"Oh, I thought I might catch a bit of sea breeze."

"You really *do* miss the sea, don't you?" asked Mavis.

"Aye," said Salty, "I do." But Salty knew the quarry work was important.

The next day, he tried to show Bill and Ben his secret with the trucks. "I like working to a musical rhythm," he said. "And so do the trucks. Why don't you give it a try, me hearties?"

"Here we go, here we go, here we go."

"No we don't, no we don't, no we don't, don't, don't."

But try as they might, Bill and Ben could not move the trucks the way Salty could.

Later that day, Sir Topham Hatt came to the quarry. He was surprised to see the job had been completed. "Well done," said Sir Topham Hatt.

"It was Salty," said Mavis. "We couldn't have done it without him."

"Then I've got a bigger job for you, Salty."

"Aye, aye, sir. What kind of a quarry is it?"

"Quarry?" said Sir Topham Hatt. "I'm sending you to Brendam Docks!"

"The *docks*?!" Salty exclaimed. "The docks are hard by the sea! Oh, thank you, sir!" he said. "This reminds me of a time in Bimini. . . ." And Salty was telling stories again.

Salty loves Brendam Docks. He gets more work done than any *three* engines and feels Really Useful. And only the trucks know his secret.

"Yo ho ho and a bucket of prawns. The tiller spins and the captain yawns."

A BAD DAY FOR HAROLD THE HELICOPTER

Harold the Helicopter loves flying.
Up in the bright blue sky, over the Island of Sodor, he looks out for anyone in distress.

Sometimes he delivers the mail. This makes Percy very cross. "The mail run is done! Is there any more? I can deliver it for you in a jiff! That's what friends are for."

"Delivering the mail is an engine's job," said Percy grumpily. Percy has many jobs, but carrying the mail is his favorite. It makes him feel Really Useful.

The next morning, Percy was happily pulling the mail train. "Must be on time, must be on time," he chuffed.

But up ahead there was trouble with the signal box. It was broken. The signal engineers did not know how long it would take to fix.

Percy had to stop. It's not safe for engines to run without signals. But Percy was very upset. "I'm going to be late," he cried, "and it's not even my fault!"

Sir Topham Hatt was in his office enjoying his toast and marmalade when he heard the news. "Percy is stuck at a broken signal? Then Harold must take the mail."

Poor Percy was still waiting. And still upset. The last time he was held up, the mail was given to Harold. "It made me feel like a Really Useless Engine," he sighed.

"Well, the mail must arrive on time," said his driver.

Just then they heard a familiar sound coming from above.
"Hullo!" said Harold. "Sir Topham Hatt says you need my help.
That's what friends are for!"

"Oh, no!" cried Percy.

But Sir Topham Hatt had made up his mind. There was nothing
Percy could do.

Percy's driver helped load the mailbags into Harold's cargo net.

"Maybe we should take the mailbags a few at a time," said Harold's pilot. "They're very heavy!"

"I'd have to make too many trips. Then I'd be as slow as Percy!"

And so they loaded all the mail into Harold's net at once. And the engineer continued to work on the signal.

Just as they finished loading, a signal engineer cried out. "It's fixed!" he said.

"Wait, Harold!" shouted Percy. "I'm ready to go!"

But it was too late. Harold had already taken off. Percy watched the mail disappear. He was upset.

But then they all heard a strange sound.
"Watch out for those trees, Harold!" cried his pilot.
"My net is too heavy!" wailed Harold.

"Harold is in trouble!" Percy cried. "We must try to help him."

"Are you all right?" called Percy.

"Just get someone to pull me out of this haystack," sputtered Harold.

And Percy did. As fast as he could.

The next day, Harold's engine was fixed and he was flying again. Percy was very pleased to see him.

"Want to take the mail, Harold?" Percy teased. "I'll stand by with the rescue team!"

All the engines tooted. And Harold hovered so low that only Percy could hear.

"Thanks for getting help to pull me out of that haystack, my friend!" he said.

"That's all right," said Percy. "That's what friends are for!"